CONTENTS

Produced by Twin Books Ltd
Kimbolton House
117A Fulham Road
London SW3 6RL

Copyright © 1992 Twin Books UK Ltd

ISBN 1-85469-954-7

Printed in Hong Kong

Hansel
and
Gretel

There was once a poor woodcutter who lived on the edge of a forest with his wife and two children, a boy called Hansel and a girl named Gretel. The woodcutter made a bare living, until the time when a great famine occurred. Crops failed everywhere, and food grew scarcer and scarcer.

One night, Hansel and Gretel overheard their parents talking in whispers. "All we have left to eat are a few dried apples," said their father. "What shall we do?"

"We must take the children into the forest and leave them there," said his wife tearfully. "Perhaps some wealthy family will take them in, and they'll be fed."

3

Gretel began to cry, but Hansel said, "Don't worry. I have a plan." Slipping outside, he filled his pockets with glittering white pebbles from the front yard.

The next morning, their parents said, "Come with us into the forest. We are going to cut wood." But Hansel and Gretel lagged behind, and Hansel dropped the white pebbles on the path so they could find their way home.

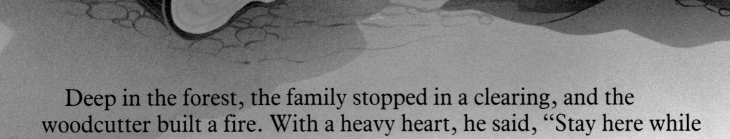

Deep in the forest, the family stopped in a clearing, and the woodcutter built a fire. With a heavy heart, he said, "Stay here while we work. We will come back for you later."

Hansel and Gretel shared the apples they had brought and took turns stoking the fire. The day passed slowly, but their parents did not return.

Worn out by worry and their long walk,
Hansel and Gretel lay down by the fire and fell
asleep. While they slept, the fire went out.

When the children woke up, they were cold and hungry. But before they could lose heart, Hansel said quickly, "Let's go and look for the pebbles."

"Oh, yes," said Gretel, jumping up at once.

The pebbles glittered so brightly that the children soon found them and took the path for home.

"How clever you are, Hansel," said his sister admiringly.

A few hours of steady walking brought Hansel and Gretel to their own familiar cottage.

Breaking into a run, they rushed into the yard, calling, "Father! Mother! We're home!"

Inside, their parents were overjoyed to hear their voices. They had been very sad since leaving them in the forest.

The woodcutter and his wife came out to greet Hansel and Gretel. But they pretended that the children had strayed away in the forest. They could not admit they had left Hansel and Gretel there.

"We began to think you were never coming home!" said their father. "You mustn't wander off like that again!"

Not long afterward, there was another great famine in the country. Again, the woodcutter and his wife lost hope of getting enough food to stay alive. "We must leave the children in the forest again," sobbed their father. "There is always a chance that they may be rescued. If not, it is better to be eaten by wild animals than to starve."

Hansel and Gretel overheard, but Hansel whispered, "I'll take some bread and drop the crumbs on the path." And so he did.

Once again, Hansel and Gretel followed their parents far into the woods. But after they had passed by, the birds came and ate up every breadcrumb that Hansel had dropped.

The forest grew dark, and Hansel and Gretel fell asleep by the fire after sharing the last of the bread.

When they woke up, Hansel and Gretel tried to find the trail of breadcrumbs, but it was gone.

"Never mind," said Hansel bravely to Gretel. "We shall just have to find our own way out."

But they walked all night and the following day without finding the right path. By evening, they were very hungry. Suddenly, Gretel shouted, "Look, Hansel! A little house all made of candy and cake!" They could scarcely believe their eyes.

17

With cries of delight, Hansel and Gretel ran to the little house and began pulling off lollipops, candy canes, and bits of frosting. The windows were made of spun sugar, and the shutters of cookies. The children were eating candy as fast as they could, when they heard a voice call from inside:

"Nibble, nibble, like a mouse,
Who is nibbling at my house?"

"It's only the wind," cried Hansel and Gretel, their hands full of gingerbread. But the next moment, they were horrified to see an ugly old woman come hobbling out. They were about to run away, but the old woman beckoned them with a skinny finger and said kindly, "Come in, my dears. I will give you better food than this."

Hansel and Gretel followed her into the house.

22

"How nice to have some company," said the old woman, peering at Hansel and Gretel with near-sighted eyes. "You must have dinner with me and spend the night."

But although she pretended to be kind, the old woman was really an evil witch who ate lost children. She had built the house of candy and cake to attract them. Then she would lock them up and cook them for dinner. Even though she did not see well, she could smell people coming a long way off.

While Hansel and Gretel had been nibbling at the house, the witch had prepared a great feast. Her table was filled with ice cream, tarts, cakes and candy, fruit, bread—everything one could imagine. Hansel and Gretel, still hungry, wanted to taste all the dishes at once.

But no sooner had they eaten than the witch snatched Hansel from the table and locked him in a cage! "And there you'll stay," she cackled, "until you're fat enough to eat."

"As for you," she sneered at Gretel, "you'll clean the house and cook big meals to fatten up your brother."

Hansel rattled and shook the cage, but it was no use. Poor Gretel was terrified. They were both so upset that they scarcely noticed the treasure hidden all over the witch's house.

Gretel had to work very hard for the witch. Every day, she drew heavy buckets of water from the stream for cleaning and cooking. And all she got to eat were the scrapings from the bottom of the pot. The witch gave the best food to Hansel, so he would get fatter.

Sometimes Gretel was so unhappy that she wished the wild animals had caught them in the forest.

Every morning, the witch went to Hansel's cage and said shrilly, "Stick your finger through the bars so that I can tell how fat you're getting." But Hansel always slipped a chicken bone through the bars instead, and the witch couldn't understand why he stayed so thin.

After a month, the witch could wait no longer. "Go to the stream for water," she said to Gretel. "Whether Hansel is fat or thin, I'm going to cook and eat him tomorrow."

"Please, don't," wept Gretel, but the witch was unmoved. "Stop your crying," she said. "That won't help you."

In fact, the cruel witch was planning to eat Gretel too.

The next morning, she said to Gretel, "First I'll make the bread. I have put the dough out to rise. Now you must open the oven door and tell me if it's hot enough to bake the bread yet." And she shoved Gretel toward the oven, intending to push her in and bake her! But Gretel had guessed the witch's plan.

"How can I tell if the oven is hot enough?" asked Gretel.

"Like this, you foolish girl," said the witch. And she opened the oven and bent over to feel the heat. In an instant, Gretel had pushed her into the oven and slammed the door!

"Hansel, we're free!" cried Gretel joyfully, running to unlock the cage. "The witch is dead!"

Hansel and Gretel hugged each other tightly and danced around the room. Then they went all over the house and filled two sacks with the witch's treasure. "Now let's get away from here as fast as we can!" said Hansel. And they ran out into the forest.

After they had wandered about for a while, Gretel said, "I think this is the path!" They followed it for several hours. But then they came to a stream that was too wide to wade or swim across.

"Here comes a beautiful swan," said Gretel.
"Perhaps she will help us." And Gretel called:
"Swan, swan, here we stand,
Hansel and Gretel, on the land.

Stepping stones and bridge we lack,
Carry us over on your white back."
And the swan kindly came to shore and took them across, one after
the other. Now they were close to home.

Their father had just come out of the cottage to cut wood when Hansel and Gretel ran into his arms. He was overjoyed to see them alive and well. The famine was over, and he had combed the countryside for news of them without learning anything about their fate.

Then their mother came out and burst into tears of happiness.

"Come in and see what we've brought!" cried Hansel.

Hansel and Gretel spilled the sacks of rubies, pearls, diamonds and other treasures onto the table. Their father stared in wonder, picking up one of the precious stones.

"This belonged to the wicked witch," explained Gretel. And the children told their parents all that had happened. They were amazed and grateful at Hansel and Gretel's escape.

"Now we'll never have to worry about money again!" cried Hansel. And he seized his father's hand and Gretel's to whirl them around in a joyful dance.

From that day, the family had everything they needed, and they lived happily together for many years in the little house at the edge of the forest.

Cinderella and the Glass Slipper

There was once a lovely young girl named Cinderella, who lived in a high stone house not far from the king's palace. Her two older sisters were jealous of her beauty and gentleness, because they were selfish and proud. They shut Cinderella out, and made her do all the work of cooking, cleaning, and mending. She slept in a tiny room off the kitchen, and her only companions were the little dolls she made to amuse herself when she had a spare hour.

One morning, the king's lord chamberlain knocked on the door to announce a great ball in honor of the prince's birthday. "All the young women of marriageable age in the kingdom are invited," he declared.

Of course, Cinderella's sisters had no intention of letting her go to the ball. While she scrubbed, they ran upstairs to find their most elegant gowns and jewels. Cinderella knew it would be useless to anger them by asking if she could attend. Besides, she had nothing fit to wear to such a grand occasion.

45

In their comfortable bedroom, the two sisters tried on every gown and cloak, slipper and sash, necklace and ribbon they owned. "I shall certainly be the most beautiful woman at the ball," said the elder.

"On the contrary," said the younger jealously, "I'm sure the prince will have eyes for no one but myself!"

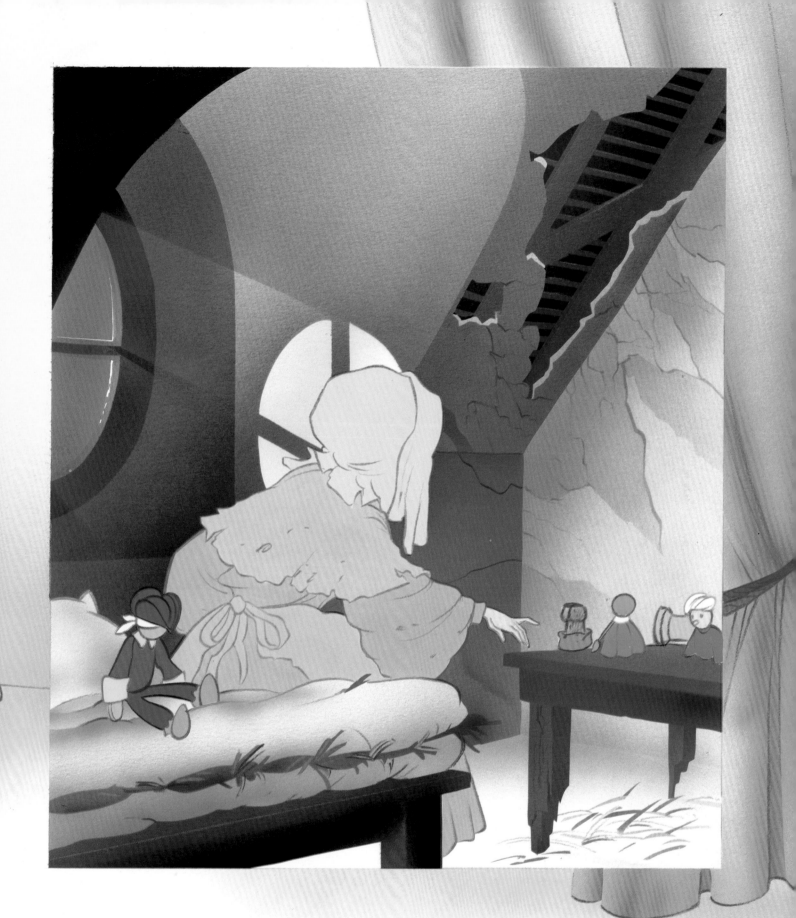

Still quarreling, Cinderella's sisters went to bed while she put out the fire, brought in the cat, and dreamed aloud to her dolls. "How wonderful it would be to go to the palace in a beautiful gown and dance all night by the light of a thousand candles." But then she laughed at herself and went to sleep.

Next morning, the whole town was buzzing with the news read aloud in the square by the king's herald: "In honor of the prince's birthday, there will be fireworks, feasting, and merriment for all. The fountains will flow with wine, and dancing bears will entertain in the streets. Besides that, there will be monkeys playing musical instruments, and a giant with a dwarf on his hat-brim!"

The country folk came from miles around to join the celebration — the biggest ever held in the kingdom.

That night, Cinderella's sisters were beside themselves with excitement. Every hair on their heads was tightly curled, and their gowns were so covered with ribbons, laces, and ruffles that they stood out a yard on every side. "My dear," they told one another smugly, "you look like a queen." For the moment, their quarrels were forgotten.

Cinderella watched longingly as her sisters stepped into their carriage and sped away through the torch-lit streets.

Turning to her dolls, Cinderella said, "Let's pretend that *we* are going to the ball." She took a pumpkin from the root cellar and mounted it on toy wheels to make a coach. Then she turned to her spool horses and said, "Now, you will be beautiful matched teams to pull my carriage. And you," she said, picking up one of her dolls, "will be the coachman!"

Just then, a bright golden light filled the dark kitchen, and a kindly voice said, "Good evening, my dear."

Startled, Cinderella jumped up to see a chubby little woman in a ruffled cap holding a wand that gave off sparkles of light.

"You don't remember your fairy godmother, do you?" asked the little woman, chuckling. "And no wonder—I haven't seen you since you were a baby. But I've watched over you in all your troubles, and now I'm here to send you to the ball." With that, she waved her magic wand, and *poof!*—the coachman doll came to life, complete with a wig and a three-cornered hat!

"Oh!" said Cinderella, almost speechless with wonder. Smiling, her fairy godmother turned to the pumpkin. Again, she waved her wand, and the pumpkin swelled up bigger and bigger, until it turned into a dazzling glass coach fit for a princess!

"And now for two footmen to ride behind and open the doors for you," said the little woman briskly.

In a twinkling, two more of the dolls came to life and sprang onto their station behind the coach.

"Dear Godmother," sighed Cinderella, "this is just like a dream. But what shall I wear to the ball?" Anxiously, she looked down at her tattered dress and clumsy shoes.

"The work of a moment," said her fairy godmother, waving her wand like a conductor's baton. And to Cinderella's astonishment and delight, she found herself robed in the softest velvet, trimmed in swansdown and seed pearls. On her feet were two small, sparkling glass slippers. Her bright hair fell below her shoulders in gentle waves, and her cheeks glowed with excitement. Cinderella's godmother was well pleased with her transformation.

"Have a grand time, my dear," she said. "But remember one thing. You must leave the palace before the clock strikes midnight, when the spell will be broken. The coach will be waiting, and you must hurry home."

"Oh, Godmother!" cried Cinderella, "how can I thank you?"

"By having a wonderful time," said her godmother, kissing her goodbye. And the beautiful glass coach rolled away toward the palace.

So great was Cinderella's beauty that the whole ballroom fell silent when she entered with the king's page. Then a murmur of surprise and wonder arose in the great hall. Who could this be?

The prince himself came down from his place with the king and queen to ask her to dance. As they circled the ballroom, the prince was captivated by Cinderella's loveliness. They danced again and again. For him, there was no other woman in the room.

At last, the prince said, "Please, tell me your name and where you live." But just then, the palace clock began to sound the hour.

"What time is it?" asked Cinderella breathlessly.

"Just midnight," replied the prince.

"I must go!" she cried, running out onto the terrace to the staircase.

In her haste, Cinderella lost one of her deli-
cate glass slippers on the stairs, but she reached
her coach just as the clock chimed midnight.

A moment later, the spell was broken. Cinderella found herself at home again, in her threadbare clothes, with the dolls and the pumpkin scattered around her.

She might have thought it was all a dream—except for the single glass slipper on her foot. Shivering with cold, but happier than she had ever been, she took off the slipper and hid it under her mattress. Just then, the doorbell rang shrilly, and she knew her sisters had come home.

Cinderella ran to the door, knowing how angry they would be if she kept them waiting. Impatiently, the doorbell pealed again, just as she turned the knob.

"Well, it took you long enough to get here!" said the elder sister. "Anyone would think you had something better to do, keeping us out in the cold like this!"

But Cinderella's other sister was still too excited about the ball to think of anything else. "My word," she said, brushing by Cinderella, "have you ever seen anything like it? Such lights! Such music! And the prince—so handsome!"

Patiently, Cinderella helped them out of their finery and saw them to bed.

The next morning, the royal herald returned to the town square. "Hear ye, hear ye!" he announced, with a flourish of trumpets. "His Royal Highness the Prince seeks news of the beautiful guest who lost her glass slipper at the ball last night!" Dozens of women flocked to the palace to try on the glass slipper, but not one had a foot small enough to fit into it. Soon the king's messengers were going from house to house in search of the woman who could wear it.

Cinderella saw the messengers coming at a distance and ran to meet them before her sisters could stop her. Love for the prince made her braver than she had ever been before. "Please, let me try on the slipper," she said to the king's men. "I have the other in my room."

Quickly, she fetched the matching slipper and slid her feet into one and then the other.

"We have found her!" cried the messengers.

The king and queen received Cinderella like a long-lost daughter, and by nightfall, she and the prince were engaged to be married. Her sisters put aside their jealousy and wished her well—so that they could be frequent guests at the palace! But Cinderella's nature was so forgiving that she never held their former cruelty against them. In fact, they soon forgot it themselves!

The whole kingdom rejoiced at the royal wedding. Nobles, merchants, and peasants alike came to wish the young couple happiness. Silently, Cinderella thanked her fairy godmother, who had smiled on her in both poverty and prosperity. She knew that they would meet again.

Cinderella brought with her to the palace the toys that had been such a comfort to her. And late at night, when everyone was sleeping, the toys would sometimes come to life again. "How good it is," they whispered among themselves, "to see our Cinderella live happily ever after." And so she did.

Snow White

Once upon a time, in a faraway kingdom, there lived seven dwarves who had a wonderful story to tell. People came from near and far to hear how they had once rescued a beautiful Princess. And when they had finished their daily work of mining gold and precious stones, the dwarves would bring out their storybook and recall just how it had happened.

Their story began on a snowy winter's evening many years earlier, as the Queen of their land sat at her window, sewing with finely colored threads.

As she sewed, the gentle Queen pricked her finger, and a drop of her blood fell on the snow-covered windowsill. The Queen had long been hoping for a child, and she made a wish. "I wish I had a child with hair as black as night, lips as red as blood, and skin as white as snow," she said.

Later that year, a lovely daughter was born to the Queen, and all her wishes were fulfilled. The child had night-black hair, red lips, and fair skin. The happy Queen named her child Snow-white. But, sadly, the Queen died soon after her daughter was born.

After a time, the King married again.
The new Queen, too, was very beautiful, but
she was proud and cold-hearted, unlike the
mother of Snow-white.

Every day, she stood before her magic mirror and asked it the same question:
"Mirror, mirror, on the wall,
Who is the fairest of us all?"
And each day, the mirror would answer:
"Of all the beauties that were, that are,
You, O Queen, are fairest by far!"
The years went by and Snow-white grew up, becoming more beautiful with every day that passed. Her stepmother began to hate Snow-white, not only because she was beautiful, but because she was kind and good and loved by all. For years, she hid her hatred from Snow-white and her father, the King.

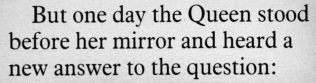

But one day the Queen stood before her mirror and heard a new answer to the question:
"Mirror, mirror, on the wall,
Who is the fairest of us all?"
This time the mirror replied:
"You are fair, O Queen,
t'is true,
But Snow-white is fairer
far than you."
The jealous Queen was enraged, and began to plot against her stepdaughter. Calling one of her huntsmen, she ordered him: "Take Snow-white deep into the forest and kill her."

The huntsman dared not disobey the Queen. Much against his will, he told Snow-white that he must go with her next time she visited the forest.

Snow-white often walked in the forest, where she could escape from the unkindness of her stepmother and the constant noise and activity of the castle. She enjoyed her quiet hours alone, but she was too kind-hearted to get the huntsman into trouble. Next time she walked in the forest, she allowed him to go with her, as her stepmother had ordered.

In a clearing far from the castle, the huntsman suddenly drew his dagger. But Snow-white was so young and beautiful that he could not carry out the Queen's order.

Confessing what had happened, the huntsman cried, "Run away! I will tell the Queen that a wild animal killed you!"

Horrified, Snow-white fled deep into the forest. Stumbling over roots and scratched by brambles, she ran until she could go no farther.

Far below, Snow-white saw a small thatched cottage nestled in a shady hollow. "Perhaps I can take shelter there," she thought. "And get something to eat before I go on." From a distance, the small animals of the forest watched and wondered.

Snow-white walked down the hill and
knocked timidly at the door of the cottage.
When there was no answer, she let herself in.

To Snow-white's surprise, everything in the cottage was very small—the cups, the knives and forks, even the beds. She poured herself a cup of milk and ate a slice of bread.

Then she lay down on one of the little beds and fell asleep at once.

Late that afternoon the seven dwarves shouldered their tools and left the mine.

In an orderly line, according to the numbers on their hats, they filed through the forest until they reached their cottage.

"Here's to a hearty meal and a good night's rest," cried Dwarf Number One. But he stopped in surprise when he saw that the cottage door was wide open.

Alarmed, the dwarves peeked inside their
cottage. But instead of a burglar, they saw a
beautiful young girl sound asleep on one of
their beds, just as if she belonged there!

"Who can this be?" the dwarves asked one another. But the only way to find out was to awaken their unexpected visitor. When Snow-white told the little men about her stepmother's wicked plot, they were shocked. Her gentleness and beauty won them over at once.

"You may stay with us as long as you like," the dwarves promised Snow-white. "Your wicked stepmother will never find you here." Snow-white was very happy to meet with such kindness after the cruel treatment she had received from her stepmother. "I will cook and clean and mend for you," she promised the dwarves. "Thank you for letting me stay." Then she set the table for dinner and they celebrated their new friendship with a party.

The next morning, Snow-white made a delicious breakfast of pancakes, fresh eggs, ham, and buttered toast. The dwarves set off for their mine well fed and in high spirits. "Now be careful of strangers," they called back to Snow-white. "Don't speak to anyone whom you don't know."

"I won't," she answered, waving goodbye.

At the castle, the wicked Queen was standing before her magic mirror.

Sure that Snow-white was dead, her jealous stepmother asked again, "Who is the fairest of us all?" She was enraged when the mirror replied:

"Queen, thou art of beauty rare,
But Snow-white, living in the glen,
With the seven little men,
Is a thousand times more fair."
Disguising herself as an old peasant in a mask and ragged clothes, the Queen brewed a deadly poison. Into it, she dipped a basketful of bright red apples.

By means of magic the Queen learned the way to the dwarves' cottage. There, late in the day, she found Snow-white.

"Good day, my child," she said in a feeble, trembling voice. "Would you like a ripe apple?"

The apple looked so good that Snow-white forgot the dwarves' warning against strangers. And her kindness made her unwilling to refuse the poor old woman's gift.

"Thank you," she replied. And she took a bite of the poisoned fruit.

Immediately, Snow-white fell to the ground as if she were dead.

The wicked Queen laughed with pleasure. "Now I need not trust my servants to obey me," she said. "I have gotten rid of you myself, and I am surely the fairest in the land."

Just as the Queen turned back toward the castle, the seven dwarves came home and saw Snow-white lying beside the spilled basket of fruit.

"Who are you?" they demanded of the old woman. "And what have you done to our Princess?"

The Queen turned and fled, pursued by the angry dwarves. They were determined to avenge Snow-white, who remained motionless on the ground.

114

The dwarves were small in body but fierce in anger. They ran after the Queen until she had to stop for breath above a swift stream. There they threw their war clubs at her and pushed her into the torrent. Her magic was no help to her. The jealous Queen was swept away, never to be seen again in that land.

The dwarves hurried home, but hope died in them when they found Snow-white lying where she had fallen. They gathered around her still form and wept. It was hard to believe that her youth and beauty had been destroyed in a moment by her jealous stepmother.

Using their great skill as metalworkers, the dwarves fashioned a gleaming casket of gold and crystal. Sadly, they placed Snow-white in the casket and set it atop a high hill. For many days and nights, they kept a vigil beside it.

One day, the handsome Prince of a nearby kingdom noticed the beautiful crystal-and-gold casket shining in the sun. He rode closer and saw that it contained a beautiful young woman.

The dwarves told him the sad story, and the Prince, too, began to weep. "She is so beautiful," he said. "Let me just kiss her once before I go."

The dwarves agreed and opened the casket so that the Prince could gather Snow-white in his arms. But as soon as he did so, her eyelids fluttered and she awoke from her long trance. "Where am I?" she asked.

Overjoyed, the Prince and the dwarves told Snow-white all that had happened since she had taken a bite of the poisoned apple.

"Come with me to my father's castle," said the Prince, "and you shall be my bride."

The dwarves were delighted that Snow-white had awakened to a new life. They danced at the wedding of their Princess and her Prince. And the happy couple never forgot the seven friends who had destroyed the wicked Queen and brought them together.

Gulliver's Travels
in Lilliput

Once upon a time, long ago, a young doctor named Gulliver was shipwrecked at sea by a violent storm. Tossed for days on the ocean's waves, with only a slim board to keep him afloat, Gulliver was finally washed ashore on a very strange land.

Exhausted by his ordeal, Gulliver quickly fell into a deep and dreamless sleep. Imagine his surprise, then, when he awakened to find that his arms and legs were strongly fastened to the ground! And his hair, which was long and thick, had been tied down in the same way.

Flat on his back, Gulliver could see only sky.
Yet he felt a soft pattering across his body, like
the footfalls of a tiny, scurrying army. And he
could hear what sounded like a hundred

hummingbirds circling round him.

Curious, and not a little frightened, Gulliver struggled to free himself. Finally, he succeeded in gaining the use of his left arm and loosening the bonds on his hair.

Rolling onto his right side, Gulliver was astonished to see a row of six-inch people armed with bows and arrows that were aimed at him!

Unable to speak the language of his captors, Gulliver did his best to signal his friendship and good will to the little people of Lilliput (for it was on the island of Lilliput that Gulliver had landed). The Lilliputians had never seen so large a man before. Although he seemed friendly, and they wanted to trust him, it was decided to take him into the kingdom bound by the ankles. There he could request his liberty from his Imperial Majesty, the Emperor.

With some difficulty, Gulliver got up and bowed deeply to the Emperor, his wife, and the court. His Majesty was impressed by Gulliver's gentle manners.

Welcoming Gulliver to his kingdom, the Emperor ordered two of his greatest scholars to instruct this "Man-Mountain" (as Gulliver was called in Lilliputian) in the language and native customs of Lilliput.

Gulliver had always been a quick learner and had studied many languages at the university. In a short time, he was able to tell the Emperor about his shipwreck. Gulliver promised that no one would be disturbed if he were allowed his freedom among the kind people of Lilliput.

132

His Majesty listened thoughtfully to Gulliver's request. Then he explained that his guest must be searched before he was released to roam freely around the island.

"Of course," said Gulliver politely.

"Here you are," said the "Man-Mountain," handing over his comb, pocketknife, watch and chain, and a wallet with some gold coins in it.

133

Now Gulliver had the freedom to explore the island kingdom from shore to shore. And what a fascinating kingdom it was!

One day the Emperor decided to entertain his huge guest with a variety of parades and shows. There were splendid performances by tiny acrobats and athletes. Then the Emperor asked Gulliver to straddle the city's Great Canal like a Colossus, while the royal barge floated beneath!

Gulliver gained the trust and affection of the people of Lilliput so completely that he was presented with a key to the city.

"As a scholar," said the Emperor, "you may wish to study the scrolls that contain the history of Lilliput."

Gulliver was delighted. He spent much time reading these old documents. From them he discovered that the Lilliputians were an ancient and proud people. Their only enemies lived on the island of Blefuscu, across the channel.

Gulliver made friends all over the city. He stopped often on his morning walks to speak to his friend Reldresal, who had breakfast on his balcony so that he could talk to Gulliver over his morning coffee.

No longer were the people of Lilliput afraid of the "Man-Mountain." In fact, it was reassuring to them to see Gulliver towering above the city.

One fine June morning, some months after Gulliver's arrival, a grand celebration was held to celebrate the Empress' twenty-sixth birthday. Gulliver paid his respects to Her Majesty and renewed his pledge of loyalty.

"Consider me at your service," he said, "in gratitude for your kindness and generosity."

Not long after this, two excited councilmen from the court came to see Gulliver.

"The Empress has sent us to tell you that we are in danger," they announced. "The Blefuscudians have launched a great fleet of war vessels! Even now, they are sailing across the bay!"

Gulliver set out at once.

Asking the local seamen about the depth of the channel, Gulliver learned that at high tide it was seventy "glumgluffs" deep—about six feet. Quickly, he waded out into the bay. The invaders were so terrified by the sight of this giant that they leaped from their ships and swam back to their own island!

Then Gulliver attached ropes to the prow of each little ship and pulled the entire fleet across the channel to Lilliput!

"Now the foolish wars between these tiny kingdoms will end," he said to himself hopefully.

At the royal port, Gulliver was greeted joyfully by the Emperor and his court. "Long live the most powerful friend of Lilliput!" they cried. Gulliver was honored with the highest title of the land, that of "Nardac."

The Empress directed that a huge display of fireworks be set off in honor of the great day of victory.

But suddenly, another disaster struck! Young Flimnap, the Emperor's favorite nephew, was so excited by the day's events that he shot a firecracker too close to the royal canopy. In seconds, it was aflame! As the people scurried to carry water and stop the spreading fire, Gulliver came to the rescue again. Soaking his handkerchief in water, he squeezed it over the flames and put them out.

151

Several days later, Gulliver was sitting sadly by the town fountain. He was very homesick, and he did not see how he could ever return to his family and friends. At that moment, a messenger arrived with bad news.

"Another warship from Blefuscu has been sighted on the horizon," he said breathlessly.

"I will go to the harbor," said Gulliver.

Walking to the shore, Gulliver marveled at the fact that Blefuscu was so warlike.

He swam over to the other island and spoke
to the King of Blefuscu.

"You are wasting your time," he explained.
"The Lilliputians call me the Man-Mountain,
and they are under my protection. You had
better stay at home."

To make sure, he put their last boat in his
pocket and returned to Lilliput.

Delighted as he was to have established peace, Gulliver could no longer disguise the fact that he was homesick. Two of the councilmen noticed his sad look and asked him, "What is wrong?"

"I miss my family and friends in England," Gulliver explained. Then he took the tiny Blefuscudian boat from his pocket and asked, "Would the Emperor let you build a boat scaled to my size, to carry me home?"

Of course, the Emperor couldn't refuse so sincere a request by his country's hero. In two weeks the boat was completed and a grand festival held to bid Gulliver farewell. He set off at high noon, waving to all his friends. As he pulled away from shore, colorful balloons rose high above the cheering Lilliputians.

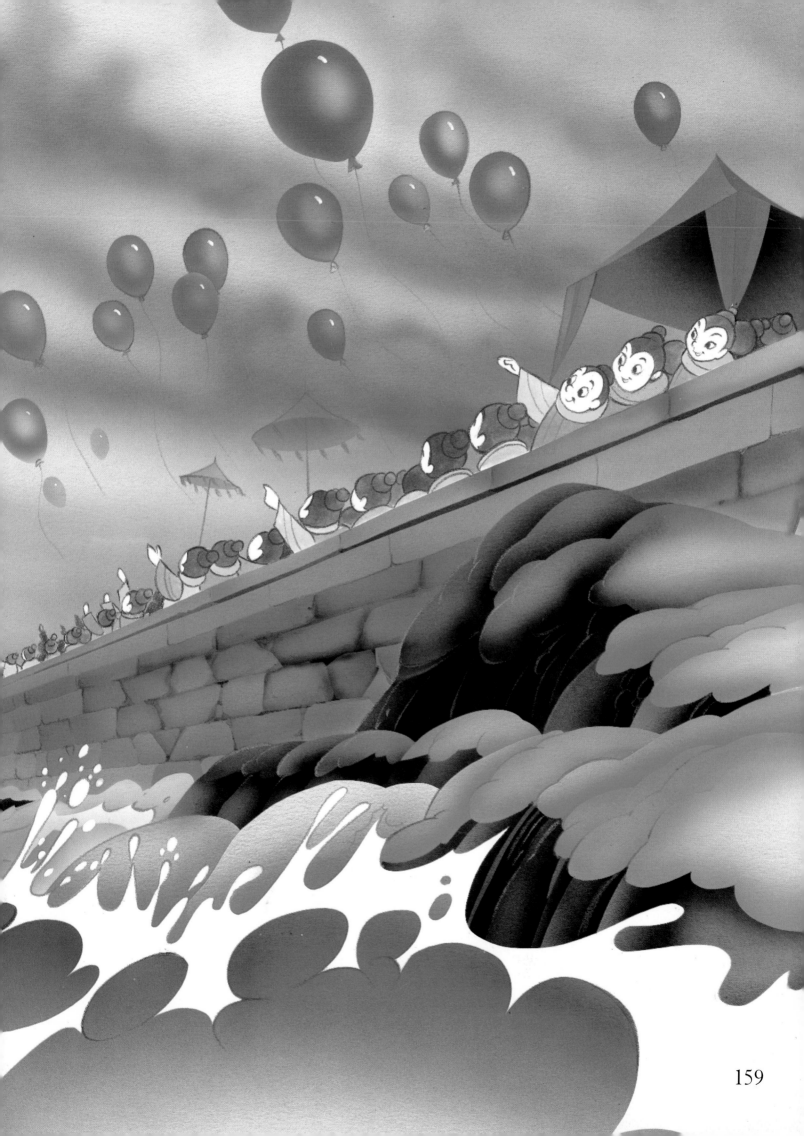

159

Two months later, Gulliver reached home. He visited the King to tell him about his wonderful journey and the friends he'd made. The King could hardly believe in an empire of six-inch people, but Gulliver produced a tiny horse and carriage to prove his story.

The King was very happy to learn of these new neighbors. He sent an ambassador to Lilliput at once. The large nation and the small one formed an alliance and enjoyed a prosperous friendship—all thanks to Gulliver's travels.

Tom Thumb

Once upon a time, there lived two peasants in a little hut in the woods. Although they were poor, they were very happy. However, there was one thing they yearned for. This was not gold or diamonds. They both wanted a child.

"I would be happy with only one child," said the husband.

"So would I," said his wife. "Even if the child were no bigger than my thumb."

In time, they did have a child—a beautiful little boy. He was blond and sweet, but very, very small. In fact, he was no bigger than a thumb. So the peasant and his wife named the child Tom Thumb.

They all lived together very happily. Tom Thumb grew older, and he learned to walk and talk and run, but he grew no bigger.

"Don't let it worry you," said his father. "The important thing in life is to be brave and good and smart." So Tom Thumb tried to be all these things, and he also tried not to be proud.

In spite of his small size, Tom was a great help to his father on the farm. When his father was plowing or hitched the horse to go to market, Tom Thumb would sit on the horse's bridle, calling commands, and the gentle horse would obey.

One day, two strangers were passing by, and saw the horse being driven by Tom Thumb. One of them thought, "We would make a fortune if we sold this little fellow to the circus. People would be astonished that one so small could command a great animal like a horse, or even an elephant."

"Let us find his father," said the other.

171

The two men told Tom Thumb's father that they wished to hire him to work on their farm. And they offered him a heavy moneybag.

"I would be a monster if I sold my child," said the father. "But Papa," said Tom Thumb, "you need the money, and I would like to have the adventure. When I have worked out my time, I will come home."

So his father took the heavy moneybag and Tom Thumb rode away with the two men.

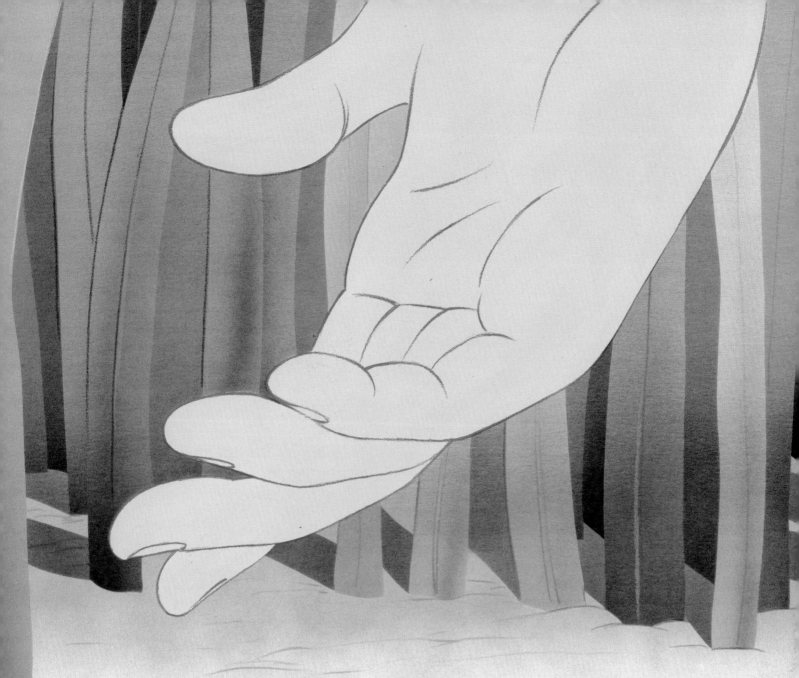

While they were walking along, Tom Thumb heard the two men discussing their plans.

"We will sell him to the circus, for a lot of money. And since the bag I gave his father was really filled with stones, we will do very well," said the man on whose hat Tom was perched.

When Tom realized they had cheated his father, he decided to run away at the first opportunity. That evening they stopped for the night, and the men put Tom Thumb on the ground while they made a fire.

Without waiting a moment, Tom Thumb scuttled into the undergrowth and hid himself under the leaves of a fern. The two scoundrels searched and called to him, but he didn't answer. When they searched the opposite side of the camp, Tom Thumb quietly hurried away.

Night had fallen, and Tom was miles from home.
"I will find my way back tomorrow," he said.
"Tonight I will stay here." And he curled up and
slept under a mushroom.

The next morning, Tom woke early and started the long walk home. Sometime later, he met two young thieves who were looking for a rich man's house to rob. Tom Thumb decided to take advantage of them and said, "I know where the rich miller lives in the next village. If you take me there, I will show you how to get into his house."

The thieves were easily fooled and they took Tom Thumb to the village, which was not far from his house. He showed the thieves a way into the miller's house. Then Tom scrambled up to the window and escaped, calling out, "Thieves! Thieves!" to the villagers. The two were captured, and Tom Thumb was almost home.

Growing tired, Tom stopped to rest in a nearby barn. It was filled with golden, sweet-smelling hay, and he decided to take a nap before resuming his journey. While he slept, snuggled in the hay, he dreamt of being home with his mother, who was singing lullabies to him.

Tom was so fast asleep that he did not awaken when the farmer's wife came into the barn. In putting a forkful of hay into the cow's manger, she put him into the manger, too!

Tom Thumb awoke as the cow took a great mouthful of the hay in which he was sleeping. Suddenly, he found himself in the cow's mouth, trying to avoid her great teeth as they ground the hay! When the cow opened her mouth to take another bite, Tom Thumb jumped back into the manger. But he wasn't safe yet, for the cow continued to eat the hay, and with each bite, she came closer.

Really frightened, Tom cried out, "Help, help!"
The farmer's wife heard a voice that seemed to come
from the cow's head and thought it was the cow
calling! Terrified, she ran for help.

She came back with the mayor, who also heard the voice calling and thought it was the cow.

"This animal is bewitched," he said. "Take it into the far pasture and leave it there until the spell is broken."

The farmer's wife took the cow to the pasture at the edge of the village, unaware that Tom Thumb rode along by the cow's ear.

Meanwhile, an old grey wolf was watching from a nearby wood. He decided that the cow would make a good dinner. As the wolf drew closer and closer, the poor cow became very frightened. But just as the wolf was about to attack her, Tom Thumb jumped off the cow's head and onto the wolf.

"Great wolf," said Tom Thumb, "you don't want to eat this skinny old cow. I know where you can get plenty of food—good food, like sausages. If you carry me to the next village, you can go and eat there as often as you like without anyone being the wiser."

The wolf was surprised, but he thought, "Many meals in peace are better than one cow now." So he agreed to take Tom Thumb to the next village.

It was midnight when they reached the village. "It is the third house after the little bridge," Tom told the wolf. "And there is a window you can crawl through at the back of the house that leads to a cellar."

The wolf crept into the cellar and soon found himself in the pantry. The table was covered with food—sausages, bacon, ham, and more. The wolf ate all he could hold.

At last he thought it was time to leave, but he had eaten so much, he was too fat to squeeze through the window. When Tom Thumb saw that the wolf was truly stuck, he called out as loud as he could:

"Papa! Mama! Help me! Help me!
The wolf is trapped in the cellar!"

It was his own house that Tom had brought the wolf to! When his father heard the voice of his son calling, he picked up a great carving knife in the kitchen and ran down the cellar stairs. But the sound of heavy footsteps scared the wolf so much that he managed to wiggle through the window and was gone.

It was a happy reunion. Tom Thumb was home—a bit bruised and bedraggled, tired and hungry, but eager to tell his parents all about his adventures.

"It wasn't easy to escape the scoundrels, the thieves, the cow, and the wolf," he concluded. "But I did, and now I'm home to stay."

199

That night, Tom Thumb was back in his own bed in his own house at last. As he went to sleep he thought about his adventures, and said to himself, "Papa was right. The important thing in life is not to be grand or to have money. The important thing is to be brave and good and smart." And then he fell into a well-earned sleep.

Beauty and the Beast

Once, long ago, there lived a wealthy merchant who had three daughters. Two of them were quite silly and selfish. They spent all their money on fine clothes and all their time gossiping.

But the youngest daughter, who was called Beauty because she was so fair, had a kind and generous nature. She saw only the good in everyone.

One day, Beauty and her sisters overheard some very bad news through the open windows. All their father's ships had been lost at sea—and with them, all their money.

Beauty's sisters made such a fuss at the idea of being poor that their father was very unhappy. He went to his bankers to borrow money, but they refused him.

The merchant went home and told his daughters, "There is only one hope of regaining our fortune. I heard today that one of my ships may have landed safely with a rich cargo. I must go to a distant port and find out if this is true."

Eagerly, his older daughters cried, "What wonderful news, Father! If the ship has come in, please bring back some new silk gowns and beautiful jewels."

"And you, Beauty?" asked her father.

"Only come back safely, and bring me a single rose to brighten the winter," she replied.

After a long, cold journey, the merchant found that his last ship had indeed come into port. He sold its cargo for a goodly sum, but on his way home he became lost in the forest.

Suddenly, a tiny purple elf appeared in the air before him. "Follow me," said the elf. And he led the merchant to the gateway of a huge palace.

As he passed through the gateway, the tired traveler was astonished to see that he had left winter behind. The walls of the palace melted away, and he found himself in a spacious hall warmed by a big fire. The elf led him through one beautiful room after another. But there was no one to be seen.

Finally, the merchant came
to a banquet hall, where the
table was set with the finest
foods. He was very hungry, so
he helped himself to the feast
and fell asleep before the fire.

In the morning, the
merchant tried to find the
owner of the palace to thank
him for his hospitality. But still
he found no one. As he was
leaving, he stopped in the
courtyard to pick a rose for
Beauty.

Suddenly, a fierce voice roared behind him, and he turned to see a frightful Beast.

"So this is how you repay my kindness—by stealing my flowers! You shall die for this!" said the Beast.

The terrified merchant fell down before the Beast and told him the story of his journey and of his promise to Beauty.

"See if she loves you enough to save your life," growled the Beast. "Let her come here of her own free will one month from today, or I will come and find you."

The poor merchant turned homeward at a very slow pace. He knew he could not hand Beauty over to the Beast.

When his older daughters came out to greet him, they were thrilled with the lavish gifts he had brought them. But when he handed Beauty her rose, he said sadly, "Little do you know what it cost." Then he told her of the Beast's command.

216

Hiding her terror, Beauty said calmly, "Of course, I will go, Father. The Beast will not harm me. Perhaps he's lonely in that great palace. But you must stay here and look after your business. I'll soon be home for a visit."

Her father's faithful horse carried Beauty safely to the palace of the Beast.

Beauty hesitated when she reached the great courtyard, but the purple elf appeared to guide her.

"This way!" he cried, and Beauty followed him into the palace, still trembling for fear of the Beast.

The elf led Beauty to a handsome bedroom filled with fine furniture. Satin hangings tied with gold cords draped the windows. On the dressing table was a jewelry box filled with priceless gems and a dozen of the roses Beauty loved.

"All these are yours," said the elf. "Gifts from my master."

Then Beauty noticed a huge wardrobe chest filled with silk and velvet gowns, beaded slippers and colorful headdresses.

Beauty took off her simple traveling clothes
and tried on one of the elegant gowns from the
wardrobe. When she looked into the mirror,
she scarcely knew herself, so grown-up and
lovely did she look.

"Truly, you deserve your name," said the elf
admiringly.

Beauty had almost forgotten her fear of the Beast—until suddenly, he appeared at her side. When she saw how huge and ugly he was, she shrank away and stifled a scream. But he looked so unhappy when he saw her distress that she calmed herself at once.

"Good evening, Beast," she said with a curtsy.

"It is good to have you here, Beauty," he replied. "I hope we can spend some time together every evening and get to know one another. It has been very lonely here for many a year."

"I look forward to it," said Beauty warmly. And so they began to meet and talk together daily. Soon Beauty looked forward to the Beast's visits, as she had no other companion than the friendly elf.

Each night, the Beast led Beauty to the banquet hall, where the table was set with all kinds of delicacies. The Beast ate nothing, but Beauty had her dinner at the fireside while they talked.

One night, as the clock chimed nine, the Beast beckoned Beauty onto the terrace. There he asked, "Did you truly come here of your own free will?"

"Yes," said Beauty. "Your kindness in sparing my father's life made me eager to keep his promise to you. And your kindness to me has made me feel very welcome."

26

"Then you shall come and go freely, as you wish," said the Beast. "But first, I must ask you: could you learn to love me?"

Beauty's heart sank, but she answered honestly, "I hope that I can."

"Very well then," said the Beast, turning away. "You may go home for awhile. But I trust you to come back in a month's time."

Beauty's father was overjoyed when she returned. In his heart, he had feared he would never see her again.

"The Beast was very kind to me" Beauty assured him. "And I have promised to go back to him." She dared not tell her father that the Beast wished to marry her. The idea was too new—and too frightening.

231

Weeks passed away, and Beauty keep putting off her return to the Beast's palace. But one night, her elf friend appeared to her in a dream. She saw the Beast with bowed head at his gateway, watching out for her return, but losing hope. Dead leaves blew around him, and he sighed deeply.

In the morning, Beauty told her sisters that she must return at once to the Beast's palace.

"What are you thinking of?" they cried. "Do you mean to leave your family forever? Stay here where you are safe, and never think of that dreadful Beast again."

But Beauty would not be persuaded. "I promised to go back, and I must," she said. "He misses me very much. I dreamed that he was growing lonelier and weaker every day."

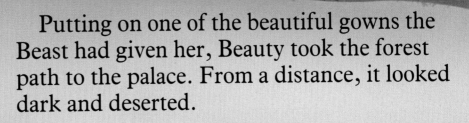

Putting on one of the beautiful gowns the Beast had given her, Beauty took the forest path to the palace. From a distance, it looked dark and deserted.

Frightened, Beauty followed the elf into the courtyard. There, as in her dream, the dry leaves swirled. But the reality was even worse than the dream. The Beast lay on the broken pavement at the point of death.

"Forgive me!" cried Beauty. "I have come back to stay as long as you wish."

"Can you really love such an ugly creature as I am?" asked the Beast faintly.

"Yes," answered Beauty. "No one could call you ugly who really knew you, as I do."

With that, a blaze of light filled the courtyard, and the Beast was transformed before Beauty's eyes into a handsome prince.

"Your love has broken the evil spell that held me prisoner as a Beast," said the prince. "Will you be my wife?"

"I will," said Beauty.

"Here is our home," said the prince, as a palace more splendid than before rose from the clouds.

The happy couple sent for Beauty's family to attend their wedding. The prince's family, too, arrived, to celebrate his release from his long loneliness.

Thus, Beauty and the prince were married, to general rejoicing, and lived to enjoy many years of happiness and peace together.